From the desk of Todd

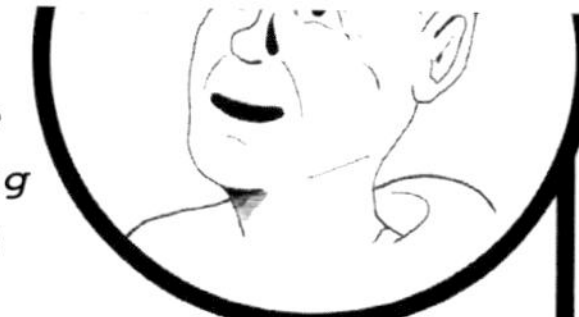

Human beings understand the people they encounter by categorizing them into buckets. Every day, there emerge new ways to organize people. We all love being a part of something in that way, but what if that "something" is shaming whole groups of people? What if the "category" you get put into is not the right one? What if you were categorized as a nerd, but you were actually a jock? What if you were labeled as "stupid" even though you had all A's? What if you were labeled as "disabled," but you really weren't? Take me, for instance. I have cerebral palsy, but my brain is just as high functioning as that of any "normal" person. My sister and my staff will be the first to tell you that I have the highest IQ!

I may have some physical disabilities, but as soon as anyone hears the words "disabled" or "special," it's like they don't know how to act anymore. I believe that our egos and expectations frequently get in the way of our feelings and love. Both are high when I meet new people because I come from a warm, loving, and inclusive family; they see me for who I truly am and do not categorize me based on my **physical limitations. The majority of people categorize** "people with disabilities" as one big group even though not a single one of us is identical to another. This makes it seem like we all have the same brain activity and physical ability as if we are all the same. We aren't! This can be particularly frustrating for somebody who may consider themselves lucky enough to have full brain function and **intelligence. It is unfortunate that it only takes someone** to glance at me before they conclude that I can't comprehend or perceive the world we share together as they do. I think that there is a big misconception about "disabled" people.

Well, I don't know if it is fair to call ignorance and generalization a misconception. To those on the receiving end, it feels like the convenient chiseling away of one's *humanity by somebody who neither understands nor has a propensity for learning about those with different bodies than they. Now when it comes to the dating world, add in a whole extra splash and flavor of challenges, difficulty, awkwardness, and more. Many people generally feel like they could never be with someone with a "disability". But really, you can be with anyone you want, as long as you feel they* ***are the right person for you. We all breathe the same air,*** *bleed the same blood.*

I've always wanted to put my life into writing, and the best way I envisioned this was by putting pen to paper and writing an autobiographical book. I didn't want the entire book to be based on my opinions alone. So, I intend to include multiple anecdotes based on real-life experiences. The people in my life, and the experiences I've had with them, have meant a lot to me. In order to protect their ***identities, I have changed the names of some of those*** *people. A book such as this requires honesty and candor. Out of respect for the many special experiences and wonderful times I've shared with a beautiful and remarkable woman I've had the privilege to know, I have made use of a pseudonym: Jennifer.*

Some people think that people with "disabilities" can't function the same way as they. They have fewer life experiences and limited cognitive function, perhaps. Take me, for instance; I can attest to the fact that whatever it is that most people assume I cannot do, I absolutely can. I am a very normal guy, and I think about the same things guys would. Not unlike your own, my life has held its fair share ***of challenges. It has been quite a challenging journey that*** *has required spirit, grit, passion, and resilience every step of the way. Needless to say, there have also been some people in my life who have helped me get where I am today. I know we all wish for and dream of the things we want and the people we aspire to become.*

I've had all of those thoughts in my head for as long as I can remember. I've pictured my lifestyle and how I want my life to look many different times, and I am still working on getting there one day. But in the long run, I truly believe having dreams to follow, and hopefully being able to achieve those dreams someday, is what gets you through life. I just wish people could understand more about people with different abilities; that we are all human, with real feelings, and have a purpose in this life just like every other person, even if they are categorized as disabled.

— Todd

I thank you!

Todd Hutchinson

FOUND OUT WE ARE HAVING A SNOWSTORM

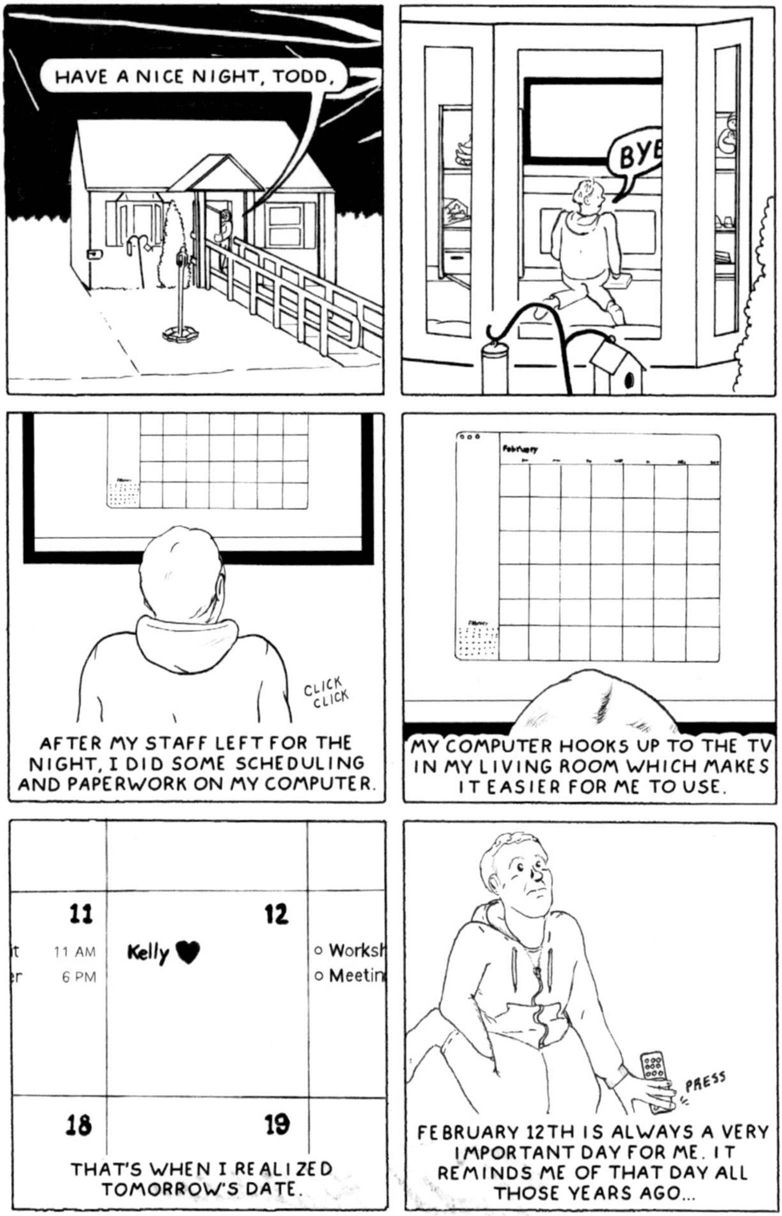

I WASN'T QUITE READY TO THINK ABOUT THAT YET,
SO I SWITCHED THE SCREEN TO TV MODE AND STARTED FLIPPING CHANNELS.
...TONIGHT'S TOP STORY, A WINTER STORM WARNING IS IN AFFECT FOR THE WESTERN NEW YORK AREA.
JUST HOW MUCH SNOW SHOULD WE BE EXPECTING?
WELL, RESIDENTS OF BUFFALO AND THE SURROUNDING AREA COULD BE LOOKING AT AS MUCH AS 3 FEET IN THE NEXT 24 HOURS.
WATERTO
BUFFALO
ERIE
BRADFORD
WILLIAMSP
THIS COULD BE A MAJOR ISSUE FOR ME.
IF I GET SNOWED IN, I CANNOT EAT OR DRINK ANYTHING UNTIL MY STAFF OR SOMEBODY IS ABLE TO SHOVEL THEIR WAY INTO MY HOME.

I IMMEDIATELY WENT TO TEXT MY STAFF.
To: Staff
Hey guys, I am worried about the weather tomorrow with the coming storm.
Don't worry about it. It's not going to get that bad out.
I know but I want to be safe
Read 10:41pm
I BARELY GOT ANY ANSWERS BACK.
IT MADE ME REALLY FRUSTRATED.
LATER, I HEARD MY CELL PHONE RING.
DING!

Wed Feb 11 10:57 PM
Jennifer
What are you doing? I miss you.
Reply
Macintosh HD
What are you doing? I miss you
Oh hey, I miss you too. I am watching TV and worrying about the snowstorm that's coming. It's supposed to get worse.
snowstorm that's coming. It's supposed to get worse.
Yeah, I'm worried too. Do you have someone there with you now?
NO

Why?
Well, I heard about the snowstorm a few hours ago. They laughed at me about it is actually coming.
Todd, they were talking about it all week and my workplace called me and they are closed tomorrow because of the snowstorm.
Really?
Really?
Yeah, and I was thinking about you and your safety with this snowstorm. I would like to come over tomorrow morning so you have some company.
You really don't have to do that.
ooo

Todd! I know that I don't have to do that but I know how you are ; you're a handicapped person. I know you might not want to admit it but you need the help especially if you get stuck inside for days. Please don't argue with me, I am coming tomorrow morning around 9 am.
OK I'm not fighting with you and I'm glad you will be here tomorrow, thank you.
You're welcome, I'll see you tomorrow morning.
WHEN I FINISHED TEXTING JENNIFER, I WAS HONESTLY A LITTLE IN SHOCK.
SHE WOULD USUALLY ALWAYS TELL ME ABOUT HER NEW MAN, BUT THIS TIME SHE DIDN'T.
ZZZ
I TURNED THE TV BACK ON, BUT I COULDN'T HELP BUT THINK ABOUT JENNIFER'S RESPONSE.
IT'S GORE-TEX
EVEN THOUGH SHE HAD ONLY WORKED WITH ME FOR A FEW MONTHS,
I FELT LIKE I HAD KNOWN HER FOR A LONG TIME...

DURING THOSE MONTHS, I HAD GROWN TO LOVE HER.
SHE SAW SOMETHING SPECIAL IN ME AND HELPED ME BE THAT PERSON.
HOWEVER, AFTER A WHILE, I REALIZED THAT I NEEDED TO GIVE UP THE IDEA OF US BEING TOGETHER.
SHE WANTED A MAN WHO DOES THE SAME TYPES OF THINGS THAT SHE ENJOYS DOING.
GOING ON WALKS, RUNNING, BIKE RIDING, GOING ON THE TRAILS THROUGH THE WOODS.
I WOULD LOVE TO DO THOSE ACTIVITIES WITH HER. I LOVE TO BE OUTSIDE WHEN IT IS NICE OUT. BUT I HAVE A LITTLE PROBLEM.
MY POWER WHEELCHAIR CAN'T DO THE THINGS I WISH I COULD MAKE IT DO.

MY PARENTS AND MY SISTER BOTH CALLED TO MAKE SURE I WOULD BE OKAY FOR THE STORM.
I TOLD THEM I WOULD BE FINE BECAUSE MY FRIEND JENNIFER WAS COMING OVER.
THEY SAID THEY WERE GLAD I HAD SOMEONE LIKE HER IN MY LIFE.
I CALLED MY CAT TO COME TO BED WITH ME.
MARTHA!
I LAY THERE IN BED PONDERING MY THOUGHTS.
zZZ
BUT I COULDN'T SLEEP FOR LONG.
CLICK
I WAS TOO EXCITED THAT JENNIFER WOULD BE HERE.

SHE WOULD BE STAYING FOR A FEW DAYS!
I JUMPED OUT OF BED AND BOUNCED ALL AROUND THE FLOOR.
I THINK I SCARED MARTHA,
!
HER HAIR WAS STICKING STRAIGHT UP.
I TOLD HER IT WAS OKAY.
I NEEDED TO FIND SOMETHING TO SAY TO HER WHEN SHE GOT HERE.
MAYBE A PICK UP LINE?
I WENT BACK TO THE COMPUTER.

Google
pick up lines for girls
pick up lines for girls
pick up lines for girls to use
pick up lines for girls on tinder
pick up lines for girls on instagram
pick up lines for girls tagalog
pick up lines for girls in hindi
pick up lines for girls reddit
CRUSHES » CRUSHES ON GIRLS
How to Talk to a Girl You Like
Co-authored by Connell Barrett
Last Updated: August 27, 2022 References Approved
WOULD YOU FUCK AN OLDER LADY?
Just send a message and ask to fuck!
VIEW PICS
BETTER THAN PROSTITUTES! THESE MOTHERS FUCK FOR FREE
NO CREDIT CARD NO REGISTRATION NO BULSHIT
SHOWMOTHERS
ADVERTISEMENT
PARTS
Part 1 Get Comfortable
1 Develop your interests. You don't need to be a brain to find things to
IT TOOK ME TO ONLINE DATING AND A HORRIBLE WEBSITE.
I WOULD BE TIRED TOMORROW.
2:47 AM
JENNIFER WOULD BE COMING IN SIX AND A HALF HOURS!

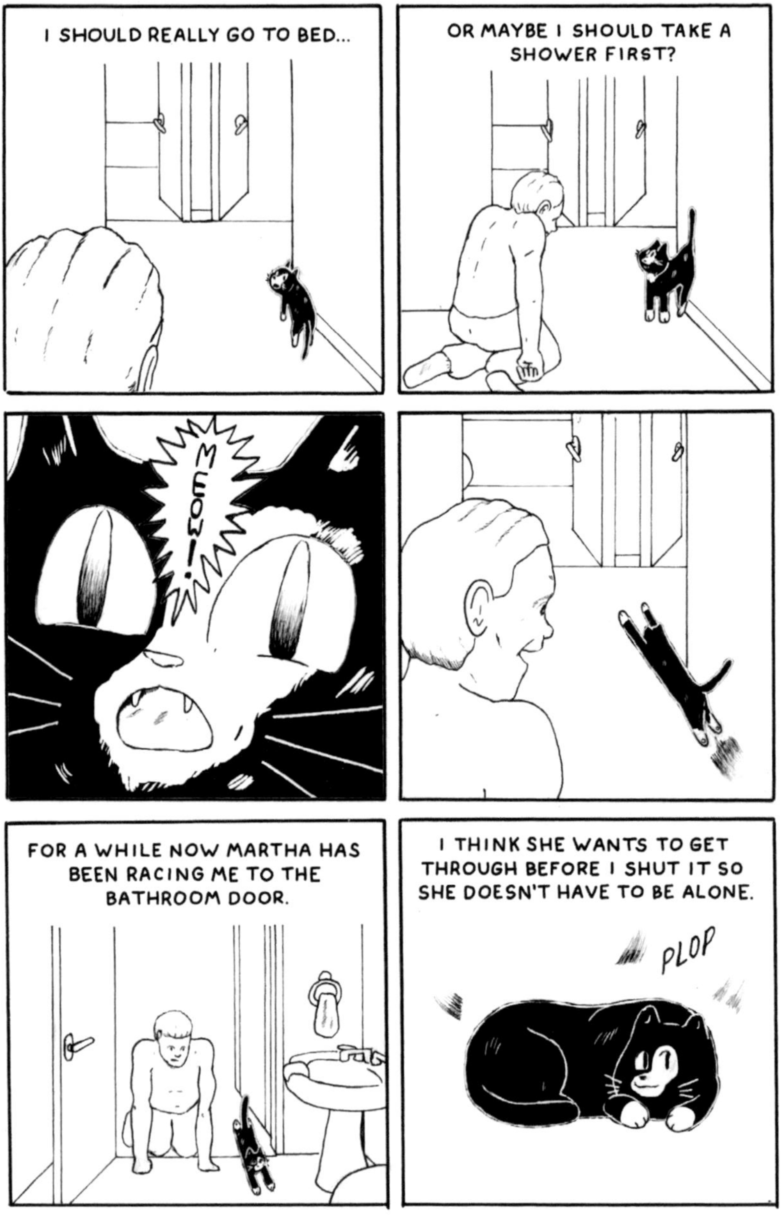
I SHOULD REALLY GO TO BED...
OR MAYBE I SHOULD TAKE A SHOWER FIRST?
MEOW!!
FOR A WHILE NOW MARTHA HAS BEEN RACING ME TO THE BATHROOM DOOR.
I THINK SHE WANTS TO GET THROUGH BEFORE I SHUT IT SO SHE DOESN'T HAVE TO BE ALONE.
PLOP

THIS IS SOMETHING I CAN RELATE TO.
C
H
MEOW?

MARTHA AND I HAVE A SYSTEM AFTER I GET OUT OF THE SHOWER.
ONCE I DRY OFF WITH MY TOWEL IT'S HER TURN.
SHE LIKES IT SO MUCH AND IT BRINGS ME JOY TO SEE HER GET SO HAPPY OVER SOMETHING THAT IS SO SMALL IN MY EYES.
PURRRRRRRRR
IT WAS ALMOST 4:00. JENNIFER WOULD BE HERE IN FIVE HOURS.
I DIDN'T BOTHER TO PUT PAJAMAS ON.

MY ALARM CLOCK WENT OFF.
BEEP
BEEP
8: 00
IT WAS FEBRUARY 12TH.
MY BED IS A HEATED WATER BED
SO YOU CAN IMAGINE HOW HARD IT IS FOR ME TO GET UP.
ESPECIALLY WHEN IT'S COLD OUTSIDE AND I ONLY HAD A FEW HOURS OF SLEEP.
I GOT OUT OF BED AND WENT TO THE LIVING ROOM TO LOOK OUT THE WINDOW.
YAWN
IN MY LIFE I HAVE EXPERIENCED MANY WONDERFUL OPPORTUNITIES,
ALBEIT SOME CHALLENGING ONES.
THERE HAVE BEEN MANY EXPERIENCES THAT I HAVE BEEN SHUT OUT FROM.
SOME I CAN BRUSH OFF AND FORGET ABOUT, BUT OTHERS STILL BOTHER ME TO THIS DAY.

ONE THING THAT HAS ALWAYS BEEN ESPECIALLY HARD FOR ME TO DEAL WITH IS MY DATING LIFE.
SINCE I HAVE A DEVELOPMENTAL DISABILITY, IT SEEMS LIKE THAT'S THE FIRST THING PEOPLE THINK OF WHEN THEY SEE ME.
I HAVE A WHEEL CHAIR, CAN'T WALK, CAN'T SPEAK CLEARLY, AND NEED HELP BEING FED AND GETTING DRESSED.
AS A RESULT, MANY PEOPLE NEVER TAKE THE TIME TO KNOW ME TRULY.
WHAT DOES THAT MEAN TO A GIRL I HAVE REAL FEELINGS FOR?
WHAT DOES THAT MEAN TO A STRANGER?
I HAVE HAD A FEW RELATIONSHIPS,
BUT THEY WERE NOTHING LIKE I WISH THEY COULD HAVE BEEN.

I LIKE TO PAUSE FOR A MOMENT BEFORE I START MY DAY AND TAKE A LOOK AROUND.
I HAVE WORKED SO HARD FOR THIS LIFE SIMPLY TO WAKE UP EVERY MORNING WHERE I AM TODAY.
IT IS A VERY EMPOWERING FEELING INDEED.
SOME PEOPLE THINK THAT PEOPLE WITH "DISABILITIES" CAN'T FUNCTION THE SAME WAY THEY DO.
SCROLL
SCROLL
1961
2012
Ted & Vicki
THEY ASSUME THE WORLD LOOKS DIFFERENT FROM A WHEEL CHAIR.
THAT WE LIVE, LOVE, AND LAUGH LESS BECAUSE OF OUR "DISABILITIES".
THIS IS SIMPLY NOT TRUE.

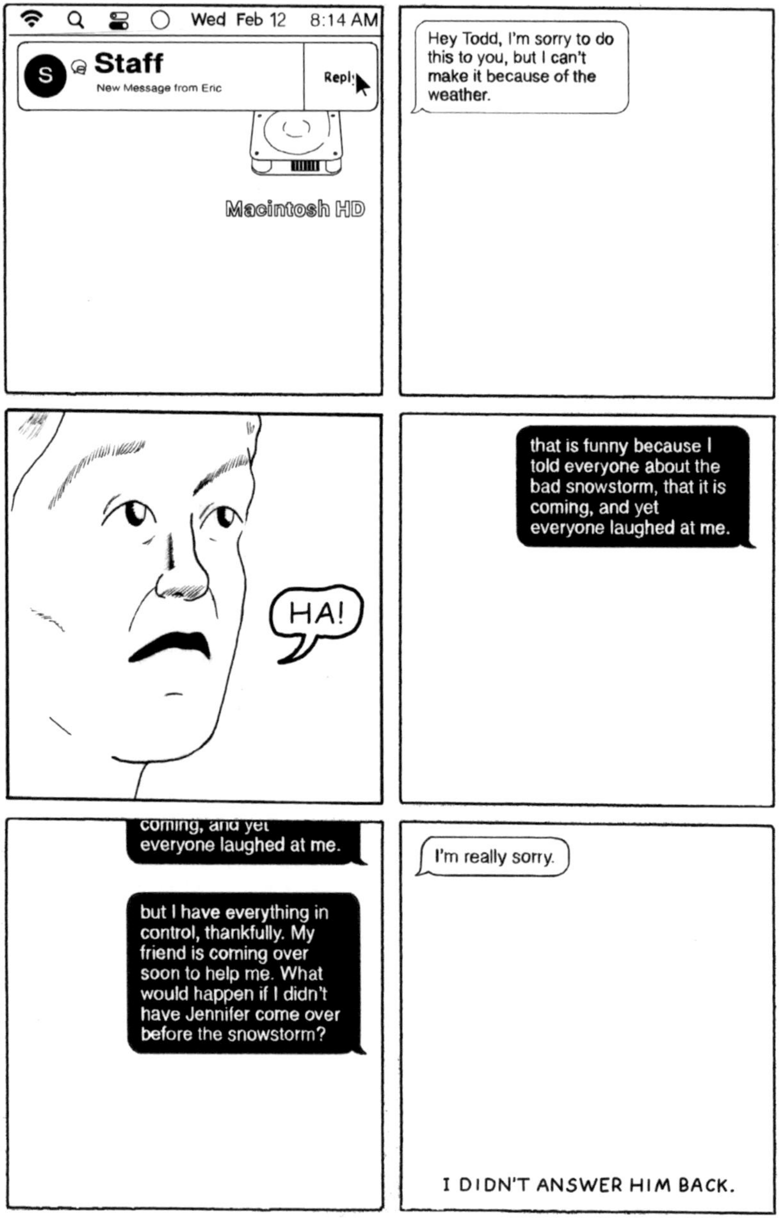
Wed Feb 12 8:14 AM
Staff
New Message from Eric
Reply
Macintosh HD
Hey Todd, I'm sorry to do this to you, but I can't make it because of the weather.
HA!
that is funny because I told everyone about the bad snowstorm, that it is coming, and yet everyone laughed at me.
coming, and yet everyone laughed at me.
but I have everything in control, thankfully. My friend is coming over soon to help me. What would happen if I didn't have Jennifer come over before the snowstorm?
I'm really sorry.
I DIDN'T ANSWER HIM BACK.

ANTICIPATION FILLED ME.
THE WIND WAS HOWLING OUTSIDE AND YOU COULD JUST TELL IT WAS EXTRA COLD THIS MORNING.
SHE SAID SHE WOULD BE HERE AT 9:00.
IT WAS ALREADY 8:21
IT FELT IRONIC BECAUSE FEBRUARY 12TH IS A SPECIAL DAY FOR ME,
KIND OF AN ANNIVERSARY.
ON FEBRUARY 12TH SOME YEARS AGO, I ENCOUNTERED SOMEBODY VERY SPECIAL.
I CAN'T HELP BUT REMINISCE NOW.
I FELT MARTHA WALKING ON ME.
I NEEDED A 20 MINUTE CAT NAP.
I TOLD MARTHA IT WAS A SPECIAL DAY.
MY GOOD FRIEND WAS COMING OVER TO HELP ME.

KNOCK
KNOCK
BLINK
BLINK
HUH?
HOW DID I GET TO THE DOOR?
WASN'T I JUST ASLEEP?
KNOCK
KNOCK
GOOD MORNING, TODD.
I'M MOVING IN!

SHIVER
SHIVER
I'M STILL IN MY PAJAMAS, HAHA.
I USE SOMETHING CALLED "AIR WRITING"
I TAKE MY HAND, AND I SPELL WORDS OUT LETTER BY LETTER.
I ALWAYS WANT TO SAY SO MUCH.
BUT I HAVE TO KEEP IT SHORT.
COME IN
DON'T MIND IF I DO!

MY AUGMENTATION DEVICE IS HOOKED UP TO THE TV.
IT HELPS ME TYPE OUT THE THINGS I WANT TO SAY.
IT SPEAKS FOR ME.
TYPE TYPE
ENTER
THANK YOU FOR COMING! PLEASE, TAKE YOUR COAT AND SHOES OFF AND MAKE YOURSELF AT HOME BECAUSE I THINK WE MIGHT BE STUCK HERE FOR A FEW DAYS.
THANK YOU TODD.
I'M HOPING THAT'S OKAY WITH YOU, TOO.
OH MY! YOU NEED A SHIRT!
SHIVER

BE RIGHT BACK.
I HOPE YOU DON'T MIND IF I LOOK LIKE A BUM.
I DIDN'T SEE THE NEED TO GET DRESSED.
THAT'S FINE WITH ME.
THERE YOU GO, THAT'S MUCH BETTER.

DID YOU CHANGE YOUR HAIR COLOR?
OH! I DID!
RIGHT AFTER I CAME TO SEE YOU LAST TIME.
I LIKE IT! I LOVE BLOND.
THAT'S WHY I DID IT.
?
I NOTICED SOMETHING ELSE ABOUT HER WAS DIFFERENT,
BUT I COULDN'T PUT MY FINGER ON IT.

OH! GUESS WHAT?
MY STAFF CALLED OFF BECAUSE OF THE WEATHER!
I THOUGHT THAT MIGHT HAPPEN.
THAT'S ONE OF THE REASONS I WANTED TO COME.
THANK YOU! YOU ARE THE BEST!
STOP THAT! I WANTED TO BE HERE, I CARE FOR YOU.
ARE YOU THIRSTY? I CAN MAKE A JUICE FOR YOU?
NOD

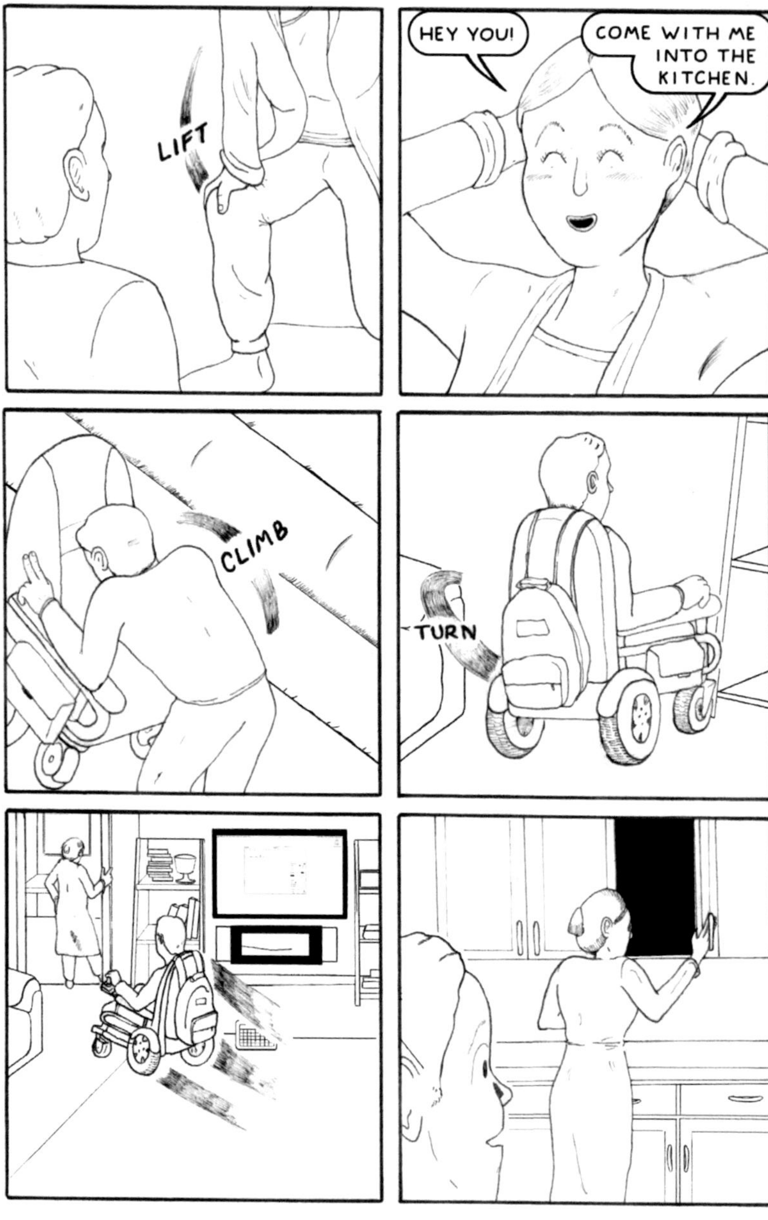
LIFT
HEY YOU!
COME WITH ME INTO THE KITCHEN.
CLIMB
TURN

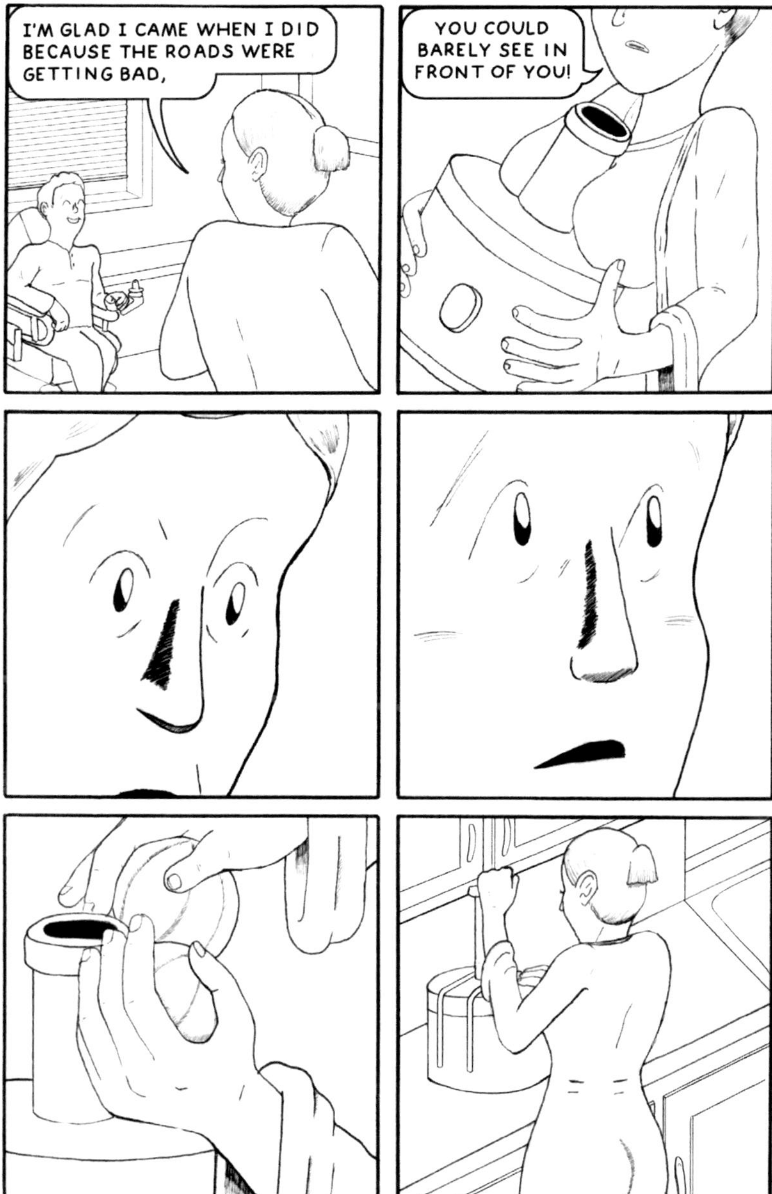
I'M GLAD I CAME WHEN I DID BECAUSE THE ROADS WERE GETTING BAD,
YOU COULD BARELY SEE IN FRONT OF YOU!

DON'T WORRY ABOUT FOOD OR WATER BECAUSE I HAVE A LOT OF IT.
OH, I KNOW.
MY TODD ALWAYS HAS FOOD HERE!
DO YOU REMEMBER WHEN WE FIRST WENT FOOD SHOPPING?
OH, YES...
YOU BOUGHT SO MUCH, I THOUGHT YOU WERE GOING TO FEED AN ARMY!
I LIKE TO STOCK UP ON DEALS, ESPECIALLY BULK ITEMS.
IT GIVES ME COMFORT KNOWING I HAVE ENOUGH SPARE FOOD IN MY PANTRY.

I HAVE TO ADMIT, I THOUGHT YOU WERE A BIT CRAZY THEN,
BUT OVER THE TIME THAT WE WORKED TOGETHER I REALLY DID LEARN A LOT FROM YOU.
YOU REALLY MADE ME A MORE JOYFUL PERSON.
I THANK YOU FOR THAT.
PLEASE STOP THAT.
VRRRRRM
VRRRRM

I COULD TELL SHE WAS LOOKING FOR MY SPECIAL CUPS.
THEY HAVE A PIECE CUT OFF SO PEOPLE CAN HELP ME DRINK.
I POINTED TO THE CABINET, TRYING NOT TO LAUGH.
POUR
JUST LIKE OLD TIMES!

CHOKE
WHOOPS!
HA HA
OH NO!
SPLASH
OH MY GOSH!
I'M SO SORRY TODD!
IT'S BEEN SO LONG
SINCE I'VE DONE THIS.
YOU KNOW THIS IS NOT THE
FIRST TIME THIS HAS HAPPENED!

WELL, I GUESS I SHOULD GET THESE SHIRTS IN THE WASH.
JENNIFER WENT TO THE BEDROOM TO CHANGE
AND I WENT TO THE BATHROOM TO CLEAN MYSELF OFF.
THWAP
I TOOK MY WET SHIRT OFF
AS ALWAYS, I WOULD NEED ASSISTANCE PUTTING A NEW SHIRT ON.

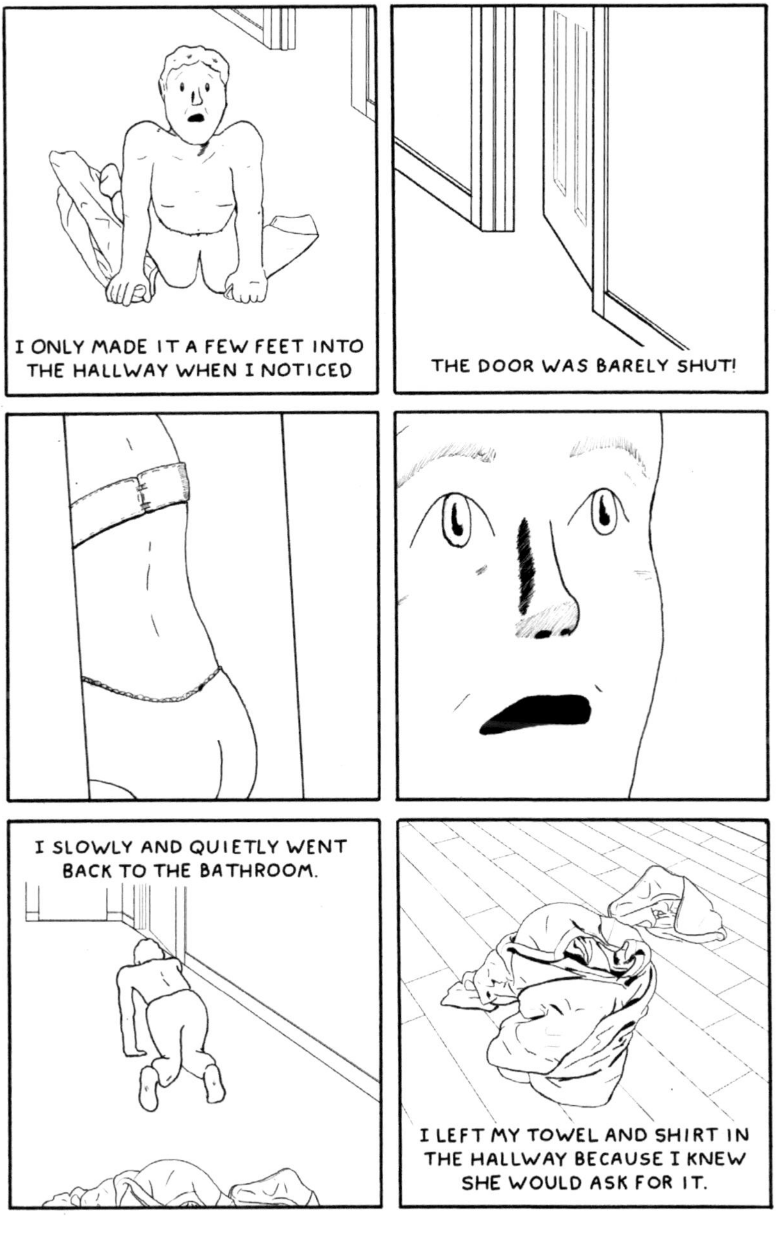
I ONLY MADE IT A FEW FEET INTO THE HALLWAY WHEN I NOTICED
THE DOOR WAS BARELY SHUT!
I SLOWLY AND QUIETLY WENT BACK TO THE BATHROOM.
I LEFT MY TOWEL AND SHIRT IN THE HALLWAY BECAUSE I KNEW SHE WOULD ASK FOR IT.

FLUSH
SHOULD I TELL HER WHAT I JUST SAW?
KNOCK KNOCK
TODD, ARE YOU ALL RIGHT IN THERE?
YEAH
HUH? WHERE DID SHE GO?
I COULD HEAR NOISE DOWNSTAIRS, SHE MUST HAVE BEEN THROWING IN A LOAD OF LAUNDRY.
I WONDER WHAT SHE'S WEARING NOW...
I MADE MY WAY BACK TO THE BEDROOM.

GREY LEGGINGS
AND A SILK PAJAMA TOP.
WHAT SHIRT DO YOU WANT?
ISN'T THAT BUTTONED
A LITTLE FAR DOWN?
POP

NO!
WHAT'S WRONG?

ITS NO-THING
OKAY...
WAS SHE PLAYING WITH ME ON PURPOSE?
HOW ABOUT THIS ONE?
THANK YOU

OF COURSE.
BRUSH BRUSH
T.V. TIME?
NOD
WHAT WOULD YOU LIKE TO WATCH?

CLICK
CRIMINAL MINDS
YOU REMEMBERED MY FAVORITE SHOW!
CRIMINAL MINDS
HUH, STATIC.
HM, I GUESS THERE ARE SOME LINES DOWN...
IT'S OKAY BECAUSE I'VE SEEN THIS ONE ALREADY.
WOAH!
WOOOOOSH

BZZT
FLICKER
OH MY GOSH!
IT'S LIKE A WHITE-OUT!
SQUINT

THE SNOW WAS PILING UP VERY QUICKLY.
YOU COULDN'T SEE WHERE THE STREET WAS,
OR EVEN MY VAN IN THE DRIVEWAY.

I HAVE A PRESENT FOR YOU.
REALLY?
WHAT IS IT?!
JUST WAIT A FEW HOURS UNTIL AFTER DINNER,
THEN I'LL GIVE IT TO YOU.

SIGH
HA HA
HA HA
HA!
SPEAKING OF EATING...
DO YOU WANT A SNACK?
I'M STARVING!
SOMETHING SMALL
OKAY, LET ME SEE.

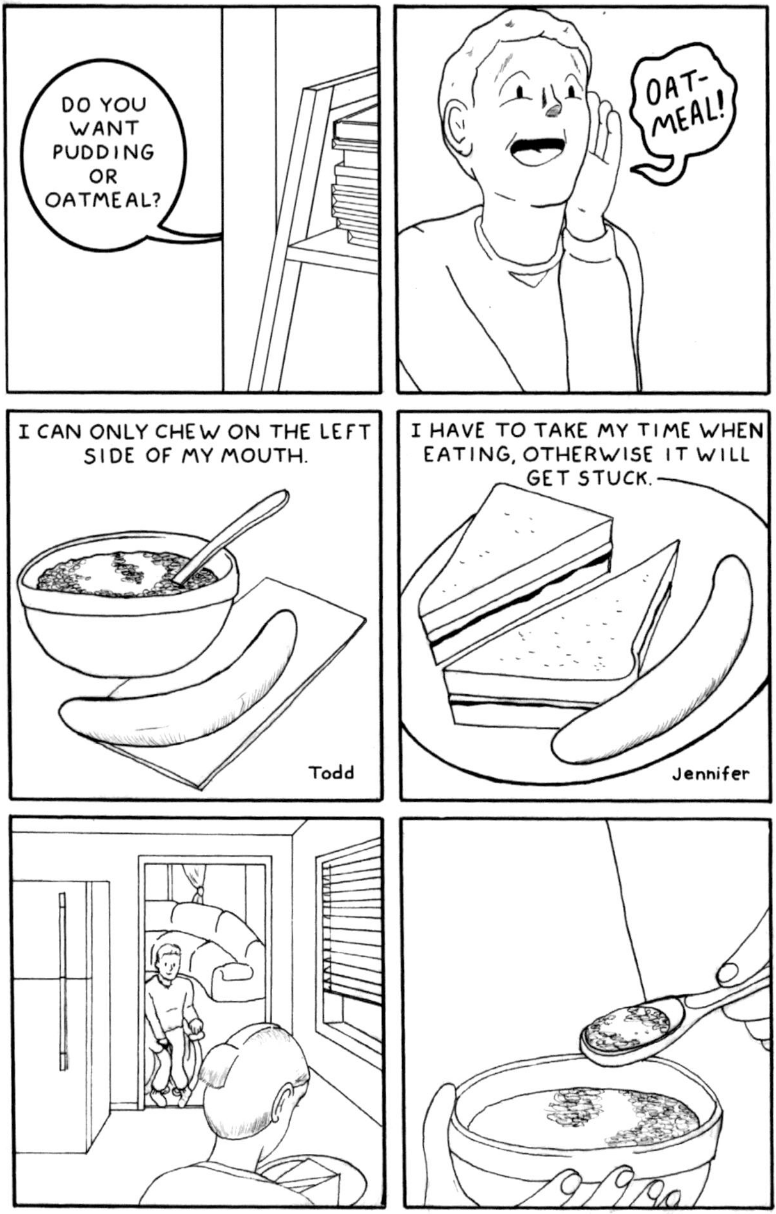
DO YOU WANT PUDDING OR OATMEAL?
OAT-MEAL!
I CAN ONLY CHEW ON THE LEFT SIDE OF MY MOUTH.
Todd
I HAVE TO TAKE MY TIME WHEN EATING, OTHERWISE IT WILL GET STUCK.
Jennifer

SO,
HOW ARE THINGS GOING WITH YOUR STAFFING NOW?
IT'S OKAY...
I JUST WISH I HAD MORE PEOPLE LIKE YOU.
I WISH I COULD COME BACK HERE,
MAYBE SOMEDAY.
HOW IS YOUR JOB GOING?

IT'S GOING OKAY I GUESS.
SHE HAS BEEN A MASSAGE THERAPIST FOR ABOUT 3 YEARS NOW.
IT'S JUST TOUGH BECAUSE MY HANDS AND ARMS HAVE BEEN IN A LOT OF PAIN.
IF IT DOESN'T GET BETTER. I'M GOING TO HAVE TO FIND A NEW CAREER.
OH NO!
YOU SHOULD QUIT.
I KNOW WHAT YOU'RE THINKING OVER THERE!
I ALWAYS THINK ABOUT HER COMING BACK TO WORK WITH ME.

WHAT ARE YOU WATCHING?
THE NEWS, I'M TRYING TO GET SOME UPDATES.
IT SAYS THERE ARE POWER OUTAGES EVERYWHERE.
THAT'S OKAY, I GUESS.
I'M NOT REALLY WORRIED,
AS LONG AS I'M HERE WITH YOU.
...
WE COULD ONLY STAND WATCHING THE NEWS FOR SO LONG WORRYING OURSELVES TO DEATH, BUT I DIDN'T KNOW WHAT ELSE TO DO!

OH!
I THINK I HAVE AN IDEA!
I LOOKED AT HER LIKE SHE WAS CRAZY.
MAINLY BECAUSE IT CAN BE EITHER REALLY GOOD OR REALLY BAD WHEN SHE SAYS THAT.
WHAT'S YOUR IDEA?
WELL, SINCE WE'RE GOING TO BE STUCK HERE A WHILE ANYWAY...
LET'S WRITE SOMETHING!
SOMETHING ABOUT YOU.
YOUR LIFE!
YOUR STORIES!
OH...

I'VE THOUGHT ABOUT DOING THIS BEFORE...
BUT I'VE NEVER ASKED ANYONE TO HELP ME WITH IT.
I COULDN'T BELIEVE SHE WAS OFFERING!
ARE YOU SURE YOU WANT TO?
IT'S NOT GOING TO BE FAST.
YES! I'M SURE!
I'LL RUN AND GET YOUR LAPTOP.
I FOLLOWED HER INTO MY OFFICE AND SHOWED HER WHERE MY PRINTED NOTES WERE.
I ALREADY HAD ABOUT 15 PAGES.

WOW TODD! YOU ARE ALWAYS THINKING.
AM I IN YOUR BOOK?
MAYBE
AND SO WE SET OUT TO TELL MY STORY.
I'LL TRANSFER YOUR NOTES AND EDIT SOME THINGS AS YOU TYPE THEM.
I.
The Beginning
SHE LEANED UP AGAINST THE COUCH BY ME AND WE STARTED.

THANK YOU TO:
ANTARA SATCHIDANAND,
D. JEFFREY HIGGINBOTHAM,
AND CRE ENGELKE,
WITHOUT WHOM THIS BOOK
WOULD NOT BE POSSIBLE.
WE ARE ETERNALLY GRATEFUL
FOR YOUR SUPPORT.

TO BE CONTINUED
IN BOOK TWO...